The Wheels on the Bus

Sandy Creek
NEW YORK

Illustrated by Polona Lovsin

The wheels on the bus go
ROUND and *ROUND*,
ROUND and *ROUND*,
ROUND and *ROUND*,

"Hooray!
Let's go!"

The wheels on the bus go
ROUND and *ROUND*,
All day long!

The wipers on the bus go
SWISH! SWISH! SWISH!
SWISH! SWISH! SWISH!
SWISH! SWISH! SWISH! . . .

"What terrible weather!"

. . . The wipers on the bus go
SWISH! SWISH! SWISH!
All day long!

"Oh no! We're going
the wrong way!"

The bags on the bus go
BUMP! BUMP! BUMP!
BUMP! BUMP! BUMP!
BUMP! BUMP! BUMP! . . .

. . . The bags on the bus go
BUMP! BUMP! BUMP!
All day long!

The bell on the bus goes
DING! DING! DING!
DING! DING! DING!
DING! DING! DING! . . .

"STOP! The luggage
has fallen off!"

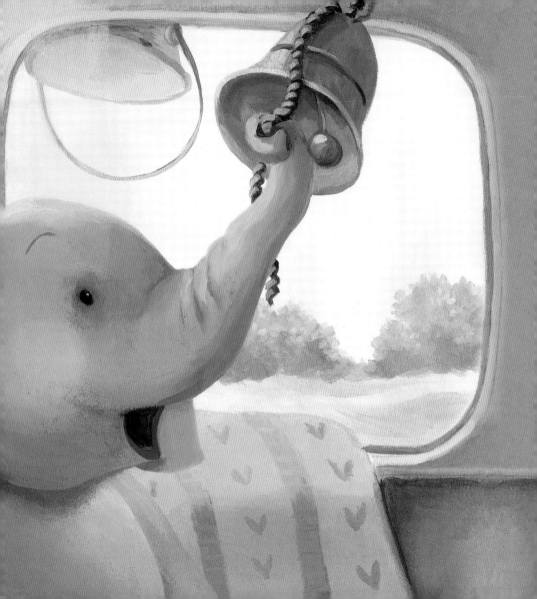

"Thank you,
Mr. Duck!"

. . . The bell on the bus goes
DING! DING! DING!
All day long!

The brakes on the bus go
SQUEAK! SQUEAK! SQUEAK!
SQUEAK! SQUEAK! SQUEAK!
SQUEAK! SQUEAK! SQUEAK! . . .

"Wait for us!"

"STOP! We've left
Little Rabbit
behind!"

. . . The brakes on the bus go
SQUEAK! SQUEAK! SQUEAK!
All day long!

The horn on the bus goes
TOOT! TOOT! TOOT!
TOOT! TOOT! TOOT!
TOOT! TOOT! TOOT!

"HOORAY!
We've arrived!"